In memory of Amechi

A Triangle for Adaora © 2000 by Frances Lincoln Limited
Text and photographs © 2000 by Ifeoma Onyefulu

CIP Data is available.

Published in the United States 2000 by Dutton Children's Books,
a division of Penguin Putnam Books for Young Readers,
345 Hudson Street, New York, New York 10014
http://www.penguinputnam.com/yreaders/index.htm

Originally published in Great Britain 2000 by Frances Lincoln Limited, London
Designed by Flora Awolaja
Display typography by Richard Amari
Printed in Hong Kong
First American Edition
ISBN 0-525-46382-8
2 4 6 8 10 9 7 5 3 1

A TRIANGLE for ADAORA

An African Book of Shapes

▼ ▼ ▼ ▼ ▼

▲ ▲ ▲ ▲ ▲

IFEOMA ONYEFULU

Dutton Children's Books ▼ New York

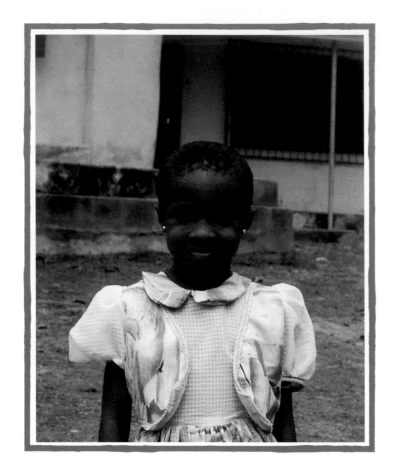

 I'm worried about my little cousin Adaora. She has been acting strange lately. She told me she liked paw-paw, but when her mother put a slice of it on Adaora's favorite plate, Adaora just stared at it.

Why won't she eat the paw-paw? If it had been a slice of orange, pineapple, or *udala* (a fruit we all love), she would have eaten it all up!

One afternoon, I asked Adaora why she wouldn't eat paw-paw.

"Because I don't want to ruin the pretty shape in the middle."

"That's a **star**," I said. "But there are lots of other interesting shapes."

"What shapes?" asked Adaora.

"Shapes like squares . . . circles . . . triangles."

"I like that word *triangle*," said Adaora.

"If I promise to find you one, will you start eating paw-paw again?"

"Yes!" cried Adaora.

So I started searching for a triangle. Easier said than done!

The first shape I found was a **square**. My big sister Uzo was using an *apkasa* to sift grated casava roots for frying.

"Is that a triangle?" asked Adaora.

"No, Adaora. It's a square," I said.

 Then I saw Uncle Eze on his way to visit his parents. He was wearing an *agbada*. Uncle Eze likes to show off, and when he saw us, he waved his arms in the air.

"Look, Adaora!" I said. "A **rectangle**."

"That's a nice shape," said Adaora. "But it's not a triangle."

Agbada

This is a beautifully embroidered robe worn by men at weddings, funerals, and many other special occasions.

Suddenly we heard drums playing nearby. We ran toward the sound and saw four musicians rehearsing for a festival. I love drums, especially big "elephant" drums.

I said to Adaora, "Look at the tops of those drums! Those are **circles**."

The musicians were good. So we listened, and when they had finished playing, we followed them.

Elephant drums

These beat out important news and make special announcements.

We were just turning the corner when I saw a little girl wearing a necklace of cowrie shells.

I pointed at the girl. "Look, Adaora. **Ovals**!"

Adaora stared, and the girl stared back. So we ran off.

Cowrie shells

Many years ago, cowrie shells were used as money, but now we wear them as jewelry, or when we pray for our ancestors.

We turned on to a path. Just then, I saw a tall *akwukwo ede* plant growing nearby.

"Look, **heart** shapes," I said to Adaora. She looked at the leaves for a long time, then agreed that they really were heart-shaped.

"But what about my triangle?" she asked.

Akwukwo ede

We use this plant in our cooking because it is easy to digest. The leaves are wrapped around grated water yam, then steamed and eaten by very young and very old people.

 Where could I find that triangle? I darted about like a butterfly, looking everywhere, until . . .

"Adaora, I see a **diamond**. Come and see."

Across the road, a woman was waiting for a bus. She was wearing a wrapper with a huge diamond printed on the front.

"I like the colors," said Adaora.

Wrappers

These are usually worn by married women, but men wear them, too, on special occasions.

 We walked on down the road. Then I saw two clay bowls on a table.

"Look, Adaora—**semicircles**! They're for sale, and they look just like the soup bowls we have at home."

"Too bad they're not triangles," grumbled Adaora. "My feet are getting tired."

We turned on to another road and saw a woman wearing four brass **rings** on her fingers. The middle ring was a special one to show that she was a chief.

"When I grow up, I'm going to wear rings on *all* my fingers!" said Adaora. For a moment she forgot about the triangle and her sore feet.

We walked on.
Then I spotted
a big plantain.
My mouth began to water.
"Hey, Adaora!" I said.
"There's a **crescent** shape!"
    Adaora said, "I'm tired.
I want to go home. You
don't know what a triangle
looks like, anyway."
    "Yes, I do," I said. "Let's
go over there. I can see a
big crowd—maybe there's
a festival going on."

Plantains

These look like bananas, but they
are really vegetables. We fry or
roast them over charcoal fires.
They taste good roasted with
palm oil and chili peppers.

 I ran on ahead, pushing between people. But the only shapes I could see were more circles and rectangles. Then suddenly . . .

"Look, Adaora— a **triangle**! I told you I'd find one. That woman is wearing the most beautiful headdress I've ever seen. It's like the one my mother made. I watched her tie it up and fix it in place with pins."

Adaora smiled and clapped her hands. "That's *my* triangle!"

The woman turned around and said, "Ugo and Adaora! What are you doing so far from home?"

It was Auntie Felicia! She gave us each a big hug, then took us home.

 The next day, Auntie Felicia sewed a pink dress with a triangle, a circle, a rectangle, and a square on the front for Adaora. Then she made an embroidered shirt and shorts for me.

Now Adaora likes eating paw-paw on her favorite plate, and triangles are her favorite shape. The trouble is, she loves her pink dress so much that she won't wear anything else. So that's something new for me to worry about!